A Treasure Chest of

ANIMAL ADVENTURES

JAZZY JOJO

authorHOUSE®

AuthorHouse™
1663 Liberty Drive
Bloomington, IN 47403
www.authorhouse.com
Phone: 1 (800) 839-8640

Published by AuthorHouse 10/04/2018

ISBN: 978-1-5462-6117-9 (sc)
ISBN: 978-1-5462-6116-2 (e)

Library of Congress Control Number: 2018911276

Print information available on the last page.

This book is printed on acid-free paper.

Dear Readers,

As you read these delightful animal stories, you will notice that none of my stories have any pictures. Their omission is not a mistake. The blank pages are inserted so that you can draw the characters and scenes as you want them to be. You are the illustrator and artist, using your very own creativity and vivid imagination to design your copy of this book, as you think it should look.

There is no right or wrong method of illustration. You have the freedom to make this book your own. Although some of the characters may have a description, you do not have to make them that way.

This is a collection of stories to be shared!

Parents and children will be able to read and discuss the characters and their behaviors, then take turns being the illustrators. You may even be inspired to create similar stories to mine, which would be fantastic!

Some of the animals have human "virtues" that we should all practice often, and others possess "vices" or negative behaviors which their friends helped them to overcome. That was done so that adult or older children could capture "teachable" moments throughout reading sessions, which may even lead to wonderful group dynamic sessions.

Thank you for giving my TREASURE CHEST OF ANIMAL ADVENTURES a try! I hope you enjoy reading each tale as much I enjoyed creating it!

JoAnne M. Saunders

*T*his book is dedicated to all of my students, (former and present), and their families. Also to all of my former coworkers both here in the US Virgin Islands and on the Mainland.

Special dedication goes out to all of my former recess club and after school activities club members, who always gave me inspiration and energy to find many creative ways to make learning to read fun and enjoyable for everyone, from toddler to 103.

As you read these stories, let your creativity and imaginations flow!

"Read it- Imagine it-Then, Draw it" make the scenes your very own!

J. M. Saunders

*T*immy and *J*immy
*L*eaping *L*izards

(by JoAnne M. Saunders)

*T*immy and Jimmy were the best of friends.

Timmy and Jimmy were lizards. Even more than that, they were leaping lizards.

Really! In the blink of an eye, they could leap in a flash from one tree branch to the next. They could quickly climb up a railing then leap back down to the floor. And they never ever made a sound! They were always very quiet.

Timmy and Jimmy liked to play outside all day long. They hardly ever got tired. When they did, they would play "Statues". That is, they'd strike a pose and stand perfectly still for a long, long time. That was Jimmy's favorite game!

Timmy liked it too, but his favorite game was "Hide and Seek". There was a very special reason why Timmy liked to play that game. He was a great hider! He knew all of the best hiding places. But not only that. Both Timmy and Jimmy had a special gift!

Whenever they played Hide and Seek, it was almost as fun as being invisible. You see, both lizard friends had something called "camouflage". That means, they had skin that changed colors to blend into the environment to avoid being bothered or eaten by other larger animals.

"Let's play Statues again", said Jimmy.

"No, let's play Hide and Seek first, "said Timmy, "then when we get tired we can play statues".

"Okay!" Agreed Jimmy! And that's just what they did!

"Tag, you're it", shouted Jimmy as he ran to hide. Timmy saw a black mat on the neighbor's porch. He crept over to it and sat very still. Jimmy looked high and low. He looked up in the coconut tree. But he couldn't find him. After a few seconds, Timmy came leaping off the mat with a big smile on his face. "Oh Boy!" exclaimed Jimmy, "I didn't see you at all. You're really good! You're turn now", said Timmy.

Jimmy saw a dark brown stairway leading up to the neighbor's door. When Timmy turned his head, Jimmy leaped onto the brown top step. Jimmy was looking all over the garden for him. But he didn't see him anyway at all. Finally, Jimmy came crawling from his hiding place and joined his buddy.

"Wow! You were terrific! I couldn't see you anywhere! Good game Jimmy, I taught you well!"

"Yes!" agreed Jimmy. "You are a great teacher and my very best friend." The two lizard friends played "Statues" in the sun for a little while. Then it started to rain, so they each ran back to their own trees for shelter. Timmy's family lived in a nice full mango tree. Jimmy's family lived high atop a coconut tree. Both were safe and dry for the night.

THE END

Jazzy Jojo

Note: This is a "Read It, Imagine and Draw It" story, designed for the reader to become the Illustrator. There's no right or wrong way to draw the characters and/ or scenery. However you, the "Illustrator" designs it is perfectly fine. Remember though, Timmy and Jimmy are lizards who have the ability to become the color of the different items they use as hiding places.

Roscoe Raccoon Learns Respect

**A "Read It -Imagine- Draw It" story book by
JoAnne M. Saunders, St. Thomas, US VI**

Roscoe Raccoon was so rude!

Nobody liked him or wanted to play with him. He was just too rude!

One day, in the forest, Sam the dog found a nice meaty bone from someone's garbage can. Just as he was about to take a bite _____ Snatch!! Roscoe ran up behind Sam, snatched the bone and swiftly pushed it inside of his favorite tree.

"Hey! That's my dinner!", barked Sam. "Now I have to go looking for something else to eat. I do not like you Roscoe! You are too rude to be my friend! Let me and my food alone!"

But, Roscoe didn't even care.

He didn't even like meat bones and he wasn't even hungry either. He just liked to make everyone mad or sad. Roscoe was a "Bully"!

Dandy Cat was playing with a ball of string she'd found in the garden. She was having so much fun pushing it and chasing it, but just as she was getting ready to pounce on it _____ snatch! Roscoe, as usual, intercepted the yarn ball, and pushed it deep inside of that tree of his. "You go get it now! Give me back my yarn! Roscoe I do not like you! You are a "Bully!" I do not like bullies at all! Stay away from me, Roscoe"! Dandy shouted to him, then sadly crept over to her family's porch and sat down to brood.

Pammy Pig was having fun rolling an ear of corn around in her fresh new mud puddle. She was so happy playing with her corn, until _____ "Zap"! "Roscoe strikes again!" he proudly yells as he runs off with Pammy's corn and, of course he stashes it into the same tree. Pammy became extremely upset and wept all the way back to the farm's pig pen. No doubt about it! Roscoe was a mean Bully!

The animals had really had enough! They called a meeting about how to stop Roscoe's bullying and stealing. "He's too rude!" shouted Sam. "He steals too much!" yelled Dandy. "I just don't like that Bully! protested Pammy.

Suddenly, Molly Cow looked up from grazing in the nice green pasture. She saw the other animals and heard their commotion, so she decided to join them to see what the trouble was.

The animals were so glad Molly joined them. She always had great ways to solve their problems. "Molly, please help us! We have a very serious problem", stated Sam.

"Yes! Roscoe is too rude and mean!" shouted Dandy Dog. "I do not like that rude Bully at all!" protested Pammy.

The animals begin to explain all of the mean things Roscoe had been doing to hurt their feelings, and how he steals from them, then laughs about it "Okay, I think I may be able to help all of you at once", Molly told them.

"Okay! Calm down. Ummm let me think! Seems like our little Bully needs to be taught a lesson", said Molly Cow. "It also sounds like Roscoe has totally forgotten about keeping the universal Golden Rule. Maybe we need to help him learn it for keeps this time."

"Awh!" Sighed all of the animals at one time. "You mean we should always treat everyone the same way we want to be treated!" Molly smiled at her friends with pride.

"Yep! That's the rule!" Molly exclaimed.

They spotted Roscoe playing all alone down by the pond. He was playing with a shiny rainbow colored ball that he had snatched from Dandy Cat's sister Cindy a long time ago. He was having a great time playing all by himself. All of a sudden, Sam the Dog ran from behind the tree and _____ snatch! Sam took the ball and ran into the yard where Bobby PitBull was lying under the farmer's car.

"Give me back my ball! I want it back now!" Roscoe yelled. But he wasn't so bold to go and take it from Bobby PitBull. So, Roscoe reached inside his hiding tree and took out his favorite stick. He liked playing fetch with that stick, all alone. Sometime he'd just sit under the tree and draw lines in the dirt with it. He rested the stick on the ground to eat his "stolen" sandwich from a neighbor's garbage can. He was soon finished, so he reached for his stick. All of a sudden, _____ "zap!"

Dandy Cat and Pammy Pig tackled Roscoe. Dandy held him down and Pammy swiped the stick. Then the two friends disappeared behind the barn. "Give it back! Bring me back my stick!" Roscoe yelled at them. They laughed at him, the very same way he had laughed at them.

All of a sudden, Roscoe began to sob loudly. All the other animals were shocked because they had never heard Roscoe cry before. Not ever. He cried and cried. He yelled out, "I don't have any friends. Nobody likes me. They knocked me down and stole my things. You guys are mean bullies!" Roscoe threw himself down on the grass under his favorite tree, and sobbed so pitifully, that the other animals began to feel badly for what they had done.

"Maybe we were too hard on Roscoe!" Sam whispered to his friends.

"I don't like acting like a Meanie!" said Dandy.

Poor Pammy was too upset to speak. She began whimpering as she brushed away tears.

Molly arrived and told the friends to go and wait by the barn. Then she went to comfort Roscoe Raccoon. "Why are you crying, Roscoe?" she questioned. Roscoe, all cried out and exhausted, answered her. "Pammy, Dandy and Sam were being mean to me. They roughed me up and stole my things! They're bullying me! They're not my friends! I don't have anybody to play with. I'm all alone!"

With that, little Roscoe started crying all over again. Molly gave Roscoe a gentle nudge and then spoke to him again. "Roscoe, you thought it was funny when you would do those very same kinds of things to everyone else. You had forgotten the Golden Rule. You were an out of control Bully. So, we all decided that we had to teach you a lesson. We just wanted you to feel the same way you had made the other animals feel. We didn't mean to make you cry."

Sam, Dandy and Pammy gave Roscoe back the ball and stick. In turn, Roscoe returned all of the items he'd stolen, including the rainbow colored ball. He handed that to Dandy. "It's not mine. I took this ball from your sister Cindy because she and her friend Stevie Squirrel wouldn't let me play," Roscoe told Dandy.

All of the friends hugged each other, and they all made a promise that there will be no more bullying. "We will always treat each other the same way we want to be treated", they promised in unison.

Roscoe felt like he had friends for the very first time. He agreed that from now on, he too, will remember to treat everyone the way he wanted them to treat him. He even began using manners, taking turns and sharing with all the other animals.

From that very day, Roscoe was not rude anymore.

THE END

Jazzy Jojo

Selfish Betty

By JoAnne M. Saunders

etty Butterfly was a beautiful Monarch Butterfly who lived in the field behind the biggest school on the island. Betty was very pretty, but she was also very selfish.

She always thought that she looked better than all the other butterflies in the field. Because of this, she felt like the others should treat her like the queen of the field. What made her feel this way? Everybody wanted to be Betty's friend. All the rest of the butterflies took turns lining up early each morning to tell her how pretty she looked and asking if they could be her friend. Imagine that!

Betty was becoming very spoiled and quite vain! She liked to eat up everybody's snacks. Whenever she got hungry, rather than fly around the flower garden to find food like the other butterflies, she'd sit perched on her favorite Hibiscus bush waiting for her two best friends Judy and Kelly to bring her some of what they had found. She did this every single time she wanted to eat. And, if they brought her something that she really didn't like to eat, she tossed it away and demanded that they go back to find her something she would enjoy. If they only had a little morsel of their favorite snack, they would hear, "Gimme some! Don't you want to be my friends?"

Judy and Kelly were really becoming like servants to this selfish demanding friend.

So for a few days, rather than visit Betty, they went to hunt nectar in another section of the vast field.

For awhile, selfish Betty didn't even miss her two best friends, because shortly after they "disappeared", Peggy and Peter joined her, on a much lower branch of the same bush, of course. No other butterfly was allowed to sit as high on the bush as Queen Betty. Betty loved to chomp on deep red or pink hibiscus petals. Peggy and Peter also liked eating them because they were sweet and full of nectar. "Come and hunt hibiscus with us, Betty" Peter urged her. "No thanks! I'm too hungry to even handle one petal", Betty answered, I'll just sit here looking at my reflection in this little puddle, and wait for you all to come back". And that's just what she did! In fact, that's what she always did every single day, all day long!

Later on, Peggy and Peter returned with the best, the largest and most delicious Hibiscus petals that Betty had ever seen. She began nervously flapping her wings to get their attention. But the two friends were too busy enjoying their snack. And of course, as usual, here comes Betty, trying to look exhausted, very hungry and pitiful.

"Me too, please! I want some, too! I said please! If you're really my friends, you'll give me the biggest petal, right?"

All four of Betty's friends were totally fed up! No! Not from eating flower petals. They were tired, angry, and fed up with Betty Butterfly! They had definitely had more than enough of her selfish and demanding behavior.

"This has got to stop!" shouted Kelly. "Betty! You are a big Moocher!" screamed Peter. Then her girlfriends joined in, "You just want to sit here while we go hunting for food!" scolded Judy. "And we're all tired of you making us do all the work and then being told you won't be our friends if we don't share with you everyday!" stated Peggy, who was usually very quiet and reserved. After stating their disapproval of Betty's selfish ways, her friends all flew away to the other end of the garden. They avoided her for several days.

The other butterflies decided to call of meeting. They really did love Betty Butterfly, but she seemed to have the wrong idea about being friends. So they made some plans to help her learn how to act more friendly. "She needs to share!" declared Judy and Kelly. "More than that! Betty forgot that friends bring something to share with each other" Peter stated. "Betty forgot the part about everybody giving something to one another. It's an exchange!" All of the friends opened their eyes wide and flabbed their wings wildly. "Yes! That's the word! Exchange!" Betty never knew how to exchange" Peggy told them. "Betty's parents think that she's so beautiful that she shouldn't have to go find her own food. They think she's so pretty that someone may try to capture her in one of those big nets and take her away from them, so they and the rest of her family always hunt for food and bring it back to her". The four friends took a few minutes pondering what Peggy told them. "Oh my! I never even thought of it that way. That's why she has to stay up so high in the bushes and trees, right?" Kelly asked.

A few days went by, and Betty missed her friends. Worst then that, she was hungry. But all of her family had already gone to hunt Hibiscus petals. She didn't really care though. She missed her friends. And she wanted something different to snack on. She decided to bravely go looking for her friends, and for some daisies and even a small mango from the tree in the school yard. She knew she couldn't carry a whole mango, but she could get a piece of the skin to bring back, then tell her friends where to find it. Just as Betty found the part of the garden that had daisies, she spotted her long lost bird friend Billy the Banana Kwit in the mango tree. Billy was a handsome bird with small bright soft feathers, a short strong beak, and an appetite for the sweetest treats in the field. "Follow me, Betty! I'll protect you! You won't get in anybody's net with me by your side."

Billy helped Betty do things she'd never done before.

Billy called to his buddies Jake the Jay bird and Sunny Sparrow to help carry a mango, some daisies, and more hibiscus back to the safe part of the field, which was becoming so populated with various types of butterflies, that it was beginning to look like a Butterfly Farm. What a wonderful scene it would be to paint!

Betty Butterfly wings were fluttering with excitement. She had her bird friends help her to arrange a party for her butterfly friends. Just when she had everything the way she wanted it, her parrot friend Pearl flew by. Seeing how tasty and colorful Betty had set up, Pearl agreed to round up Betty's butterfly friends and tell them of the party. "Awrk! Butterfly Party, come this way! Butterfly Party, follow me, Awrk!!" Pearl announced throughout the field.

When her four friends showed up, they could hardly believe their eyes. "Oh, Betty! We've really missed you so much!" cried Judy and Peggy. "We only wanted you to stop being selfish and learn to share", they told her.

"And boy-o-boy! You really learned your lesson!" Peter chimed in. "With this feast for us, we have to give you an A+, Betty"! Kelly stated and all the others joined in. The friends were very happy and proud that Betty had learned to share and become such a great friend to all of them.

Pearl Parrot led the entire band of friends in a cheer. "Three cheers for Betty! Hooray! Hooray! Hooray!"

From that day forward, Betty Butterfly gladly shared her snacks and became the very best friend any creature in the field could ever have.

THE END

Jazzy Jojo

Turbo Tyson

Written by JoAnne M. Saunders

Tyson was a Terrapin. That means he was a land turtle. But, he was not like most people believe turtles to be. Tyson was far from slow. He was very fast! In fact, he was so fast that everyone called him nicknames like "Speedy", "Swifty" and so on. But the title Tyson liked most was "Turbo".

"Yes! That's who I am! Just call me Turbo Tyson!" He'd proudly declare. Tyson wasn't just fast. He was pretty strong for a turtle too. His legs were thick and sturdy. He also had a large flat round shell that could hold almost three times his weight. That came in handy around the forest.

Tyson had lots of friends who often called upon him to help them out. Lola and Lottie Ladybugs would always hitch rides on Tyson's back for a ride to their favorite rose bush. Terrence Turtle, one of Tyson's little brothers, would beg him to "drive" him to the orchard, where they would sit and eat wild berries. Even Bonnie Blue Jay would asked him, "Hey Tyson, Please carry these twigs over to my new nest for me?"

"But, wait a minute!" Tyson exclaimed. "You can fly faster than I can crawl, and you're stronger than me, too."

"I know it!" replied Bonnie, "But I just thought that since you like helping the others, I'd let you help me sometimes, too." Then they both had a great laugh together.

Tyson was a kind turtle. He didn't mind helping his friends and making new friends when they needed his help. In fact, he enjoyed it. He liked it a lot. Helping others made him very happy!

One bright and sunny summer day, Tyson was busy playing with his two little brothers, Terrence and Tariq. The three of them liked to play in the meadow by a huge lake. As usual, the three turtles were holding another racing competition. Of course, being not only the oldest, and swiftest of the three, Tyson usually won most of the time. But, nobody seemed to care. It was all just for fun!

Tyson loved hearing all of his friends cheering "Turbo Booster! Go Tyson Go! Go Turbo Tyson! Go Turbo Go!" This would propel him to go full speed and victory was his once more.

As Tyson and his brothers finished racing and Tyson took his victory lap, they heard something strange. Someone or something was crying out and calling for help. "Quiet!" whispered Tyson. "Someone is in trouble and needs our help. Let's go and see!"

It was a little boy. Seems as though some of the children had been playing kick ball, and the ball rolled into the lake. Doing as little boys often do, Peter ran into the lake to get the ball. But the ball landed further than the boys could safely wade. It landed in the middle of the lake. Realizing it was too far away, Peter turned around to return to shore, but his pants leg got stuck on something, and he began to panic. He fell down and was too afraid to move, but his friends kept shouting for him to just stand up so that the water would only reach his knees.

Tyson wanted to help. But, the child was far too big to get on Tyson's back. Besides, Tyson was a land turtle so he could not swim. He pondered for a moment, as the other boys tried to calm their frightened friend. Suddenly, Tyson saw his friends Suzy Swan and Daley Duck playing on the other side of the lake. Actually, they were playing with Peter's ball, rolling it back and forth to each other. Tyson found a napkin on the ground, he waved it to Suzy, who came over to the edge of the shore right away. Daley had Peter's ball in his mouth. He quickly shook his head, throwing the ball back on shore. Frankie, one of the other boys, picked it up and held it tightly. "Sorry, Peter! We didn't know it was yours!" Daley said. Suzy Swan saw that Peter was stuck. She quickly lowered her long neck into the water and used her beak to free Peter's pants cuff from the rock it had gotten tangled on.

A greatly relieved Peter was finally able to speak again. "Oh, thank you! Thanks for helping me! It feels so good to have you all as my friends", he told them. "Well, if you really feel that way", chimed Tyson, "let's all play some ball!" Peter, Frankie, and the other boys looked at each other.

Frankie dropped the ball, and faster than a Jack Rabbit, Tyson used his nose to bat the ball to Daley Duck, who kicked it to Terrence Turtle, and then it rolled to Tyson's brother Tariq.

"What a strange, crazy sight this is!" exclaimed Suzy Swan. "Whoever saw such a mixed up game as this one?" Shaking her head, she continued. "Boys, turtles and a duck playing ball together! This is too wild for me!" And with that, Suzy Swan swam back down the lake.

Just then, Tyson Turtle used his front right foot to kick the ball with all of his might. The ball rolled past all of the other players, and Tyson sped past all the bases as everyone screamed and chanted "There goes Turbo Booster! Go Tyson Go! Turbo Tyson strikes again!"

THE END

Jazzy Jojo

Ballet For Birdie

(Based on a true story)

Ms. Miles' dance class had a new pet. Actually, Birdie belonged to another teacher. However, whenever Ms. Miles put on her favorite ballet music, Birdie would squawk and squawk loudly, until Ms. Miles raced down the hall to bring his cage into her class.

Birdie was no ordinary Cockateel! He was very talented. He was also quite funny, too! This bird actually had definite choices he'd like to hear when music was played. He hated Rock & Roll, with few exceptions.

He loved classical music best of all. But, without any doubt at all, Birdie's favorite musical selection hands down, was Tchaikovsky's Nutcracker Suite, most especially "The Sugar Plum Fairy's Theme".

Whenever Ms. Miles played the Ballet Warm-ups CD, Birdie would sit on his perch, as if in attention. Moving his little head side to side, right in perfect time with the music. Some of the ballerinas would giggle to themselves. Ms. Miles would just smile. When it was time to practice isolation routines, Birdie would balance himself in the middle of his perch and raise his wings, according to which arm the girls were instructed to raise. At first, everybody though they were just imagining it. Then Ms. Miles moved Birdie's cage closer to the table where she and the girls could keep an eye on this mysterious "Ballet dancing" bird. Ms. Miles decided to give this unusual "dancer" a little test. She let the girls move beside the table that Birdie's cage sat on. First, she put on the Sugar Plum Fairy selection.

Just as before, the girls raised their right arm, Birdie raised his right wing. They moved their left arm. He moved his left. They did a head roll, he moved his head from right to left, and they moved two steps to the right. Standing in the middle of his perch, Birdie moved his tiny feet to his right. When the dancers moved left, so did Birdie. When they did turns, he flew around his cage in the same direction.

"This is incredible!" exclaimed Ms. Miles. "Let's see if he likes to Jazz dance also." The young dancers began practicing their Broadway dance routine, and again Birdie did the correct moves in the appropriate directions as they did. When the music stopped, Birdie began squawking and carrying on louder and louder.

"He's angry with you, Ms. Miles!" Laura chuckled. "Yes! Ms. Miles, Birdie's mad with you for real!" giggled Joanie.

"Okay! Settle down!" Birdie continued to protest until he heard his favorite tune again. Ms. Miles played Sugar Plum Fairy and as instantly as the music began, Birdie took his place in the middle of his perch as the dancers sat down and fixed their eyes on him, in pure amazement. This magnificent Cockateel actually performed the entire ballet routine, from start to finish, then bowed his head when the music ended. The whole class began to clap and cheer for Birdie. They all began chanting "Birdie Ballerina", "Sugar Plum Birdie", "Ballerina Birdie!" And this crazy bird actually seemed to love all the attention and recognition he was getting.

Birdie was the "Special Guest Performer" for the next several weeks on those Saturday morning dance classes. Then, after a while, one morning, as Ms. Miles opened the door of the rehearsal room, it was totally quiet! There was no squawking! Fearing that something had gone wrong with Birdie she rushed down the hall to Ms. Walter's classroom. The cage was there, but it was empty. Birdie was gone.

As Ms. Miles turned to walk back down to her room, she noticed a new poster on the wall. It was a schedule titled "Birdie". There was a list of Ms. Walter's students' names and the weekends and holidays each child would get the pleasure of taking Birdie home with them. "Oh, so that's it!" Ms. Miles muttered to herself, slightly disappointed.

The ballerinas began arriving, and they too noticed that it was more quiet than usual. Immediately they began to panic, thinking that something had happened to their favorite dancing pet. "Settle down, girls! Birdie is fine, just not here!"

"What happened to him?" asked Laura. "Who took him?" Shouted Joanie

"They better bring Birdie back to us! He's our "Star Dancer!" exclaimed little Nancy. "We miss him!" "We want him to come back, Ms. Miles" the young girls lamented and started to cry.

"Settle down, girls! You are all forgetting something very important!'"

Remembering the first day she had brought this annoying loudly squawking Cockateel into her rehearsal space, Ms. Miles reminded them.

"What did I tell all of you repeatedly? C'mon, think hard!"

Suddenly they all looked around at each other, pondering the message they were told to remember several weeks ago. "What did you tell us, Ms. Miles?" asked Laura "We were so excited to have Birdie, I guess we really weren't listen much!" she confessed.

"Okay then. Everyone line up and follow me!" their teacher ordered them. "Follow me, ballerinas!" As the girls entered Ms. Walters' room, they saw the empty cage and the Birdie Schedule on the wall. Suddenly, Laura realized what her teacher was trying so desperately to make them all recall. Almost, all at once, the tearful dancers recited out loud what they should have remembered "Birdie does not belong to us! The only time he's at school over the weekend is when there's no student in Ms. Walter's class to take him with them for a visit."

After a momentary pang of sadness, the ballerinas composed themselves enough to start their rehearsal. Ms. Miles hooked up the CD player, arranged her musical selections for the day's practice. Then ordered the tiny dancers to their assigned group lines. After the usual count down of 5-6-7-8 the first routine commenced. It was The Sugar Plum Fairy! "This one's for Birdie", Laura announced.

THE END

Jazzy Jojo

Millie, Tilly, Lily and Willie

(Written by JoAnne M. Saunders)

When Millie, Tilly, and Lily were baby birds, some pesky, pestering, unfriendly pigeons chased their parents away. Such a terrible thing to happen to these three tiny birdies! But one day, while she was struggling to fly down for some nice bread crumbs, Lily met Willie. Willie was so strong and very brave. He wouldn't let any of the larger birds bother those three precious little girl birds at all.

Whenever Eddie Pigeon, Tom Thrushie or any of those rude Seagulls appeared, looking for trouble, Willie would let out a loud squawk for his buddies to help him chase those bullies and trouble makers away. Then he always would take some tasty potato chip, bread or cracker crumbs up to the three birds' nest. Though he never entered their tiny home, Willie always stood watching somewhere close by to make sure everything was alright. Millie, Tilly and Lily felt very safe and happy that Willie was their protector.

Soon the three birds outgrew their tiny nest. Willie began scouting around for longer twigs and stronger twine. He also found several long pieces of straw. The girls' nest needed to be wider, longer and stronger. Willie proved to be very helpful to them.

He'd fly up to them, carrying straw in his beak. If Lily and her sisters liked it, they'd add it to their new home. But, as the girls began wrapping, shaping and weaving bits and pieces together, if Willie brought them a twig, or straw they did not like, they would toss it out forcefully, sending the building material straight to the ground. Poor Willie would then have to circle the whole neighborhood, seeking the best length, weight and texture to add to the nest. Most of the time, Lily and her sisters would grin and flab their wings with approval of his choices. This made Willie extremely happy!

The three bird sisters had finally finished building their brand new nest. They proudly invited Willie to come and see all that they had done. Willie was as respectful as he was shy. He never actually entered their home, but instead, he only poked his head in and looked around.

All of a sudden, Robby Robin appeared on the scene. He never asked permission, and just swooped down, entering the three sisters' brand new home. "How rude! Get out of here Robby." screamed Millie. She was very upset!

Robby liked to tease. He had no manners. He never said please or thank you for anything. Robby flew around and as they chased him, he backed up, shook his tail in Willie's face, then left the nest. Fearing that Robby would return later, Willie decided to camp out on the roof above the nest for the entire night. He was right.

When Robby thought that Willie was gone, he tried to enter the three girl birdies' nest once again. In a flash, Willie flew off the roof and pounced down on Robby's back with all his might. A stunned Robby flew away without a fight. It appeared as if he had learned a good lesson.

Millie, Tilly and Lily were all safe once again. Willie felt quite proud of his courageous act, and they all flew down on the ground together for a feast of potato chips and bread crumbs. They were having a terrific time!

In a matter of minutes, something strange started to happen!

The sky became very dark, almost like night. Actually, it was as if someone had stolen all of the island's sun and replaced it with deep ugly clouds. Willie led his three friends to a dry, safe place in the stump of a huge tamarind tree. The bird sisters were so afraid, but not Willie! He kept them warm and dry by covering them with the sleeve of an old ragged flannel shirt. Suddenly, trade winds became high pressure cyclonic gusts. Heavy rains seemed to pour down almost forever. It was certainly a full, head-on category 5 hurricane. "S-s sounds like the whole world is crashing down around us outside"! exclaimed a visibly frightened Millie. "I'm so scared"! cried Tilly.

"Don't cry and don't be afraid, girls! Willie's here to keep you safe! As long as we stay inside until all the winds stop, we will be just fine, so don't worry" Lily wasn't scared nor worried. She fell fast asleep.

The winds stripped all of the neighbors' trees bare. Branches, leaves, fruit, poles, lights, roofs, pieces of folks' walls, and all sorts of belongings were strew all over the place. Whatever didn't blow away, floated away in massive gallons of sea water. What a nightmare!!!! The little island took a real beating!

Finally, after several hours, it was daylight and the birds could go back out again.

As they all flew around cautiously, surveying all of the destruction, Millie, Tilly and Lily came upon a vaguely familiar sight amongst the rubble.

"Oh no!" shouted Lily. "Our nice new nest!" Exclaimed Millie. "Looks like there's only one thing left to do" chided Tilly.

Without another moment's thought or pause, Willie gathered up a long strand of straw. Millie, Tilly and Lily took their usual places within the roof's rafters. And they all began the task of rebuilding their nest. In no time at all the job was completed.

Willie politely stood at the entrance, admiring the brand new home.

"Are you kidding me, Willie?" Lily asked. "Get in here, Big Brother!" Millie told him.

"If it weren't for you, Willie, I don't know where or how we would have survived that storm", Tilly told him.

Willie felt his heart flutter! He liked being called Big Brother.

He also liked, though it never came to his mind before, he really liked being the member of a family. Especially this family! He had gotten used to being alone, but that didn't mean that he enjoyed it. Feeling sort of strange and funny all over, Willie turned and flew back out of the door. Then before the three sisters knew what was happening, Willie flew back inside and shouted loudly, "Hello girls! I'm home!"

THE END

Jazzy Jojo

Cali The Calico Cat

WRITTEN BY JoAnne M. Saunders

CALI Cat lived in the state of California, which is why most people thought her owner called her Cali. But, no! That's not how she got her name. Her owner, Jalesha, named her Cali because she's a Calico Cat.

Calico cats have beautiful colors all over their bodies. Cali's head had patches of tan, black, dark brown and white. Her back was tan and black. She had a black front paw, and a tan paw. Her left hind leg was white and the right hind leg white with a brown patch but both feet were blonde.

Many of the neighbors seem to be afraid of Cali, but Jalesha thought she was beautiful. Cali followed Jalesha everywhere she went. Jalesha's friends had mixed feelings about her pet. "Why is she so mixed up and ugly?" questioned Clarence. "I think she's beautiful!" exclaimed Benny.

"She looks all patched up like a jig saw puzzle!" teased Darcy. "If she was mine", joked Alfred, "her name would still be Cali, but it would be short for Calamity!" Then they all had a great big laugh. All except for Benny.

Jalesha was upset! "I don't care who doesn't like you, Cali! You're my cat and I love you! If nobody else does, that's just too bad for them. They're not my friends! Only Benny because he likes you, too!" Jalesha picked Cali up into her arms, and went to her room. She gently placed Cali on her favorite satin pillow, then fell across the bed and began to cry.

When Mom called to her, Jalesha dragged herself down to dinner. Mom could tell that something was wrong and that her little girl was sad, or mad. "Okay. What happened with you and your friends this time?" Jalesha started to cry all over again and told her mother the entire story.

"Remember, Jalie (Mom's nickname for Jalesha), beauty is in the eyes of the beholder. We look at Cali and see a truly gorgeous animal. Others see her as almost a mistake of nature. Sorry, but I'm afraid we really can't control how other people think or feel about different things in life. We can only control how we react to their opinions. It's just another one of those sad facts of life that I talk to you about, Sweetie Pie!" Mom hugged Jalesha sympathetically, and Jalesha went outside to relax and cool out in their porch swing.

As she started to feel better, Benny came riding by on his bicycle.

"Darcy and Clarence are cruel", Benny told her. "They think everything that's not just one solid color is ugly. Don't let them get to you!" He parked his bike and slowly walked up the porch steps. "Can I have a swing, too?" he asked her. "Sure you can!" Actually, Jalesha was glad for some positive company after the run-in with those other jokers.

When the street lamp outside her house came on, Benny jumped back on his bike and zoomed down the road to his house. Jalesha could see his porch from hers. She waved at him when he ran up his steps. He waved back, and Jalesha took Cali with her upstairs to get ready for bed.

But, as she reached the top of the stairs, she remembered that she didn't have to go to bed just yet. As a matter of fact, Mom had said she could stay up as long as she wanted because "tomorrow is a holiday".

"Oh boy!" shouted Jalesha with glee, "We can stay up and watch TV all night if we want to". She hugged her pet, and turned to the "Cats 101 Show" which came on the new 24 hour Pets channel. They always watched all the cat shows together. Jalesha tried several times in vain to get Cali to do some of those neat tricks the cats on TV did. But, Cali would just sit on her favorite satin pillow, and watch the TV screen nonchalantly. Cali was just contented with being Jalesha's pretty Patchwork Calico Cat.

The next morning, Jalesha woke up to hear a big commotion outside. As she sprang out of bed, and looked down the road, she saw red lights flashing from the ambulance, and the siren was blasting. There were so many people crowded around the victim, she couldn't see who the emergency workers were tending to. Mom had gone to see what was happening, as she told Jalie to wait on the porch. Jalesha collapsed into the porch swing, and a skittish Cali leaped into her lap.

Jalesha began swinging. And Cali started to meow uncontrollably, as if trying to tell her something.

After about an hour, Mom slowly walked, almost creeping, back down the road.

She climbed the steps, almost in a trance. Jalesha was afraid to ask what, why or who the ambulance had come to get. She was hoping that none of her friends or schoolmates, or anybody in their families had gotten hurt or were in danger. Unfortunately, her mom's words would sting worst than a Wasp.

"What on earth happened Momma?" Jalesha braced herself for the answer, but she really wasn't as sturdy as she thought. Mom grabbed her close and, with tears in her eyes whispered, "Clarence and Darcy were playing a very foolish game up on top their roof. Darcy dared Clarence to try to dive off and land into their swimming pool. Clarence hit the ground."

The truth was almost too much for Jalesha to bare. True, Clarence had hurt her feelings by laughing about Cali, but he was just teasing. They had shook hands at school during recess and he had apologized for talking badly about Cali. "Oh no, Momma!" Jalesha cried. She was too afraid to hear the rest. She jumped up and ran up the steps to her room. Mom was able to regain her strength and go to her room. The cheerful house had been transfigured into a place of sadness within minutes.

After about an hour of endless agonizing bawling, Jalesha got up the courage to inquire about her classmate's condition. She went into the kitchen, and sat down as Mom set the table for lunch. "The tuna macaroni salad looks good, Momma", Jalesha told her. "After the morning we had, I really didn't feel like cooking today" Mom told her. Jalesha reached into the cabinet and got out the crackers. "This is just right" she told her mother. "Jalesha, I was too upset to even tell you but I got a call from Clarence's dad a while ago. That boy is so lucky and very blessed!" Mom stated. "He'll be almost completely healed after a while. But, he's going to be unable to walk for at least the next two months" Mom informed her. "He won't be playing much basket ball or base ball any time soon, if ever again". Jalesha wanted Mom to just tell her straight out why Clarence couldn't walk, or play ball for a long time. Before she could get up the nerve to ask, Momma shouted "He just had to take that dare, so now he has both legs broken in two places. He'll be lying in bed for a long time, then have to use a wheelchair, and eventually a walker, then finally a cane."

They were so busy discussing Clarence's predicament, that they didn't notice that Cali was missing. "Cali, Cali, Cali" Jalesha called as she searched each room of their house, then she went to the front porch, and then the back yard. No Cali! Cali was not there!

Jalesha searched the neighborhood, looking in all of Cali's favorite hiding places. Finally, scared, confused, and even a little annoyed Jalesha stomped into the house shouting, "Cali! You come out from where ever you are right this minute!" But, Cali didn't appear to be anywhere nearby! Cali had vanished!

"Now, one thing for true", Mom told Jalesha, "Cali is very smart, talented and independent. Most cats are. They only stick around you as long as they want to. Cats are their own bosses. You'll be able to find her only if and when she's ready to be found. Trust me, Sweetie, Cali is neither lost nor stolen. She'll come back when she's ready. You'll see."

Days went by, and Jalesha missed her pet so very much. She turned her TV to Cats 101, but had to turn it off because every cat on the show took her thoughts back to Cali. Two weeks past, and still no sight of Cali. Even more strange, neither Benny nor Darcy had seen her outside either. They all searched the whole neighborhood several times. They went door to door asking the neighbors. Finally, they decided to stop looking for Cali and just patiently wait for her to come home on her own.

"Hey! When are you coming to see me?" Clarence asked. He called her to inquire. "I thought we were great friends now! By the way, thanks for sending your funny looking cat to keep my company. And guess what? She really isn't ugly at all! I said that because I was jealous. Thanks so much, Jalesha, for letting Cali come over to keep me from being sad and really feeling lonely. She's a great companion! And you're right, Jalesha! Calico cats are truly beautiful. Especially Cali! She's terrific!"

THE END

Jazzy Jojo

The Lonesome Little Ground Dove

By JoAnne M. Saunders

Gilbert was a gentle, shy little Ground Dove. Somehow, when Momma and the other doves flew to a brand new nest, Gilbert got left behind.

There were many other types of birds on the school's roof and in the school yard, but none like Gilbert. There were plenty of birds in all the school's trees and in the garden, but not like Gilbert.

Gilbert was different. He was brown and tan. His body was almost the same shape as pigeons, but he was much smaller. And he certainly didn't look like any of the seagulls or sparrows either. And he certainly could never resemble the Thrushy birds at all. No, he was the only Ground Dove at our school. All the others had flown away.

Every day, the children would count the varieties of birds which came to eat their spilled snacks at lunch time. On any given day, you could see at least twenty pigeons. There'd be about five or six seagulls, maybe a couple of sparrows, yellow Sugar birds, a half dozen Thrushies and even one or two Hummingbirds. And then you'd see Gilbert! And he was always all by himself.

One afternoon, Gilbert decided to try to find some new friends. The pigeons were very bold and proud. They were strutting up and down the corridor of the school. The students had spilled popcorn, and that was the pigeons favorite snack.

As they munched the fluffy corn kernels, Gilbert shyly walked over to them. "Hello, I'm Gilbert" he announced.

"Hey, Charlie! Look at this funny looking little bird," Peter Pigeon teased. They made a circle around him, as if to play a ring game. But, they were not ready to play with Gilbert at all. "Get outta here, Kiddo! You are too little and you do not look like us. You're too ugly to hang with us. Fly away before you get hurt!" Peter told him.

"I think my feathers look pretty", Gilbert answered sadly. "I look like my mother and brothers." Gilbert protested. "So, where are they then?" chided Tommy Pigeon.

'He's so ugly, they all flew away and left him here!" Johnny pigeon added and all of the pigeons teased him badly and laughed wildly.

Gilbert felt so embarrassed until he flew back up in the bush where he had made his own nest and he cried himself into exhaustion. "I will try to find a friend again tomorrow." Gilbert told himself.

The next day, Gilbert decided to try to make friends with the beautiful seagulls practicing how to fly up high then swoop and dive for fish on the waterfront near the school. He began imitating their movements. When he had perfected them, he flew over to introduce himself.

"Hello guys! I'm Gilbert Ground Dove and I'm all alone. Can I be your friend?" All of the seagulls stared disapprovingly.   Some of them mocked him. One of the gulls gave him a sympathetic smile and waved him over.

"Listen Kid", Chris Seagull answered, "You can't keep up with us over the sea and across the ocean". Seeing how disappointed Gilbert was, another gull added, "Look little guy, we fly over the sea and across the ocean most of the time, and we eat fish." Still another sea gull protested, "Look at you, then look at us! You are very different. Your feathers are short and brown with tan highlights. Your feet and beak are too small to catch sea creatures, and you can't go over deep water like all of us! Sorry Gilbert!" With that, the Seagulls all flew away.

Gilbert was all alone once again. He felt so lonely and lost. He missed his Mom and his brothers. He began to realize that none of the other birds wanted him around. Even worse, some of the school boys would hurl stones at him whenever they felt that there were no adults watching them. The little girls seemed to like him and even drop crumbs on purpose for him to eat. But when the school days ended, and all of the children went home, Gilbert always found himself by himself.

Each night, he cried himself to sleep because he was suffering from loneliness. But, one day, while Gilbert flew to the back gate of the school, he saw something. All of a sudden he realized that he had never flown to that area of the school before. He began to scout around and explore the new territory. He had never seen so many plants, flowers, and pretty butterflies before.

But, wait a moment! Were his eyes playing tricks on him?

He thought he had caught a glimpse of another Ground Dove. But when he looked again it was gone. "Just wishful thinking, I guess", Gilbert told himself. He reluctantly headed back towards the school's basket ball court. "Oh no! I'm seeing things again!" Gilbert told himself.

But it was not his mind or eyes playing tricks on him. There was a whole flock of Ground Doves in the middle of the pigeons. After a few minutes, Gilbert again got enough courage to go over and introduce himself. Once again, he took a deep breath, then spoke "Hello! I'm Gilbert! I'm all alone and I have no friends. My family flew away and I got left behind. Can I please stay with you all?"

As he braced himself for yet another rejection, Gilbert heard something entirely different this time. The prettiest bird he'd ever seen before flew over to him and said, "Hello! I'm Goldie Ground Dove. This is my family." Then, she called the other doves over. "Here's Momma, Papa, Jill and Bill".

Gilbert felt like he belonged with these birds. He so wanted to stay with them. He felt happier than he'd been since his family flew away.

"Gilbert! You will no longer live alone! No! You must come live with us!" Momma said it almost like a command. "It's not good for you to be alone, especially around bad boys who like to throw stones at us" Goldie announced. "There's plenty of living space in our nest among those bushes, and there's another nest also on the school's roof. You come and live with us."

Suddenly, Gilbert Ground Dove had a family, he had nice friends, he felt safe and most of all, he felt loved. From that day on, Gilbert would never feel lonely again.

THE END

Jazzy Jojo

Timothy Turkey and Friends

Timothy Turkey was worried. Timothy Turkey was upset. Even worst, he was scared!

"What's wrong, Tim?", his animal friends inquired with puzzled looking faces.

"Autumn's here! Can't you feel it in the air? Those Humans call it Fall because of how the leaves on the trees change colors and fall off. Just look all around this yard! Yes, it's Fall all right!"

"So, what's the problem? Why does that bother you, Timmy?" asked Scooter Squirrel. "Yeah!" chimed Ricky Raccoon, "Why does that bother you? I think the leaves are pretty!"

"Why don't you like Fall, Timothy?" His farm friends kept asking. "And, why on Earth are you so frightened?"

"Because, I'm a turkey! It's one of the worst times of the year for me. Don't you all get it? I Am a Turkey!" and with that, Timothy flew away to his hiding place, in tears.

The other animals felt so sad for Timothy Turkey, but they still didn't understand what he was trying to tell them, or why he felt scared. They sat around the yard together, pondering the situation. Suddenly, they all began staring at each other, and as their eyes grew wider than ever, in unison they screamed, "Oh No! Timothy is a Turkey!" It's as if they all finally felt the horror Tim was pondering, all at once. And as that reality began to sink into their little brains, all of Farmer Bill's farm animals began to cry.

"Poor Timothy!" cried Lisa Lamb, "he's afraid he'll end up like his cousin Tom".

"That would be so dreadful!" sobbed Ronnie Rabbit.

As the animals tried in vain to comfort each other, Daphne Duck and Goldie Goose waddled up to them.

"What's all this fuss about so early in the morning?" quacked Daphne. "Gracious sakes alive!" exclaimed Goldie. "Who died?"

"Nobody yet, but maybe Timothy will be gone soon! It's Autumn and we all know what that means, right?" And with that, Ronnie Rabbit and Lisa Lamb started sobbing all over again.

"Have you all forgotten something? We are all farm animals, so we are all in danger of losing our lives to those heartless Humans, from time to time", stated Daphne in a philosophical manner. "Most of my family is already gone!" declared Goldie.

The farm friends all huddled together, then slumped down as if to shelter each other in a crisp cool pile of freshly fallen leaves. The air had that first chill of Fall in it, which put them all in a bittersweet mood. The farm was silent! The animal pals were in deep thought. They wanted to save their buddy.

"Thanksgiving, Christmas, New Year's Eve dinners, parties, I hate those Human holidays so much!", shouted Ronnie Rabbit.

"Because, we're endangered, too! Wait until Spring comes around! Easter, Mother's Day. I'm just as afraid as Timothy is right now", stated Lisa Lamb.

The animals napped and thought and cried, then thought some more. Timothy had gone into hiding. He had no idea that all of his friends were trying to help save his life.

"I bet they don't even care! Just wait until after these "holidays" when I'm no longer around! Then, they'll miss me! They'll be looking all around for me, and nobody will ever find me again. First, I'll be the main dish and then become "left-overs". Just like the rest of my family members. Maybe, if I starve myself like last year, I'll still be too thin to go to slaughter again. Yeah, I just won't eat so much until holidays are over".

In the meantime, the other farm animals pondered how they would save Tim from becoming Thanksgiving or Christmas dinner, at least for this year.

"I got it! The perfect solution!" exclaimed Roger Raccoon. "We could disguise Timothy as another type of a bird! Clever! Right?"

"Okay", chimed Goldie Goose "exactly what did you have in mind?"

All of the friends popped up and listened with excitement.

"All we need to do is make him look like something those Humans don't want to eat", stated Daphne Duck.

"Yes! It may be a bit difficult though, because some of those creatures eat almost anything that's meaty and plump", added Goldie Goose.

"What about an ostrich?" suggested Ronnie Rabbit.

"That won't work", complained Lisa Lamb, "His legs are way too short".

"We can fix that! Use your, ah what they call it? Roger, help me out here. What's that word humans say all the time? Imagine? Oh! Imagination!"

By this time, Timothy had cheered up just a little, and headed back to join his friends. As he approached them, he saw them all gathering huge piles of brightly colored leaves. Roger Raccoon scurried off in a huff and returned with a bundle of assorted feathers. Then he and Scooter Squirrel speeded off again, and this time returned with something the Humans use to stick stuff together.

The animals were so busy bustling around with all kinds of crazy ideas, and gathering items for Tim that they didn't even notice him in their midst.

"Hey, you crazy guys! What's going on here?" Timothy chided.

"It's all for you, Timmy, my boy! Did you really think that we were just gonna let you suffer through this season all alone without even trying to help out?" Daphne exclaimed.

"Timmy, what we have here is called 'camouflage'!" stated Roger Raccoon.

So Timothy's friends took turns applying the glue, then rolling him in the leaves, and finally placed the feathers all around his body. When they had used up all of their "disguise supplies", they proudly stepped back to view their creation. All of the farm animals, including Timothy were amazed.

"But he's still too short to be an ostrich!" declared Daphne Duck.

"But he looks like a magnificent Peacock! He's so beautiful!" Goldie Goose chimed gleefully!

After spending time in the sunny section of the yard, to make sure that the glue was totally dry and that Timothy's disguise would last until the end of Fall, they took him down to the lake so he could see his reflection.

As Timothy's eyes got a glimpse of his new disguise, he began to strut around like a Peacock he'd once met.

"Wow!" He exclaimed. "Is this really me?" Timmy breathed a sigh of relief, then said "Thank you all! What wonderful friends I have!"

And the animal friends all began to cheer, march and dance! Timothy Turkey was safe!

THE END

Jazzy Jojo

Animals On Parade

Mrs. Swanson's class was having a very serious discussion.
It was about animals. "You know", started Hakim, "I just don't understand why real circus animals never come here."

"Me neither", agreed Makeba. "And why don't we have a zoo on our island? Where are the elephants, lions, bears, and tigers?"

"Oh! I'd love to see a panther or leopard up close" chided Tasheda.

"And, why don't we ever have any giraffes down here? I'd love to see one down here", she sighed. "Our weather is almost like Africa's. So, why no zebras either" Shekita added. "I'd love to pet a zebra."

Mrs. Swanson tried to calm down her class, but the questions kept on coming. Finally she told them "Alright! It's true that we have no zoo, nor does the circus come down here. But, where I come from there's a zoo with animals from all over the world. I'm not too sure that all of the animals are happy, though. They need special food, provisions, heaters in their cages for winter, even blankets to be wrapped around them on bitter-cold nights. I'm afraid our local government here couldn't afford the expense."

"But, why doesn't the circus ever come here?" Peter asked.

"I guess bears and elephants don't like to fly" replied Henry.

"Perhaps monkeys and show ponies get sea sick if they're on the barge too long", added Amylou. "Well, all can say is it's such a shame!" shouted Donzie.

"Now class, true we don't have zoos or the circus. But, we do have the Sea Life Conservatory and a wide variety of other animals that statesiders very seldom get to see." stated Mrs. Swanson.

As the class quieted down, Mrs. Swanson put on a video about an American circus show. It began with a grand animal parade through town. The entire class seemed to really enjoy it. After the movie, Keith raised his hand and asked "Why can't we have our own animal parade?"

At first everyone began to giggle uncontrollably. Then Marcie raised her hand and asked, "Hey, why can't we have one?" Suddenly, all the wild laughing stopped. Marcie continued, "I can pull my cage of rabbits in my wagon. I have three of them. Bon Bon, Don Don and Fluffy".

Makeba spoke next, "Darla is my Siamese cat and I can push her in my doll carriage." Suddenly, the entire class began making plans for what was about to be the best animal parade their school and community had ever seen. Mrs. Swanson sent out letters to the parents, and town leaders. All of the students helped to make brightly colored posters to advertise the event and invite the entire school body. And while one set of students took care of registering schoolmates and their pets to be in the parade, others passed out fliers to schoolmates and neighbors. The entire neighborhood seem to be looking forward to this parade.

Finally, parade day had arrived! All of the students were so excited!

People were lined up on both sides of the street along the parade route. No school on the island had ever had an animal parade before. Makeba's mom had invited the Governor and the entire Legislature. There was a special reviewing area set up for them, right at the school's entrance.

Hakim's dad, Officer Linden, provided a police escort up the center lane of the road. Rush hour was over, so no one would be inconvenienced. Everybody was in place. Spectators had all taken their seats. "Show Time!"

With the blowing of Conch shells, and the beating of drums, as well as music blaring from Mrs. Swanson's SUV, the parade began amidst cheers from the onlookers. Behind Officer Linden was Grand Marshall Mr. Swanson. Then came Keith dressed as a Ring Master, complete with a real Top Hat. He was riding on his pet donkey, Diablo. Behind him, marched Marcia with her wagon of rabbits. Behind her was Makeba with her cat Darla dressed in a baby onesie and bonnet. Darla even looked comfortable lounging in the doll carriage. Sheketa surprised everyone when she marched by with her terrier Buffy, and her poodle Ginger who wore rhinestone studded collars. Buffy and her pets were all dressed in identical leotards and ballet tutus. The audience went wild!

Henry rode on his Pinto pony Sunny. Peter marched proudly with Barnie his lamb. Then Tasheda rode by on her pet goat Yanni. Only she could ride her goat, of course. Shawn carried a cage containing Tullie, his giant turtle. Tiffanie-Ann's cage contained two iguanas from the palm tree in her backyard. Oscar's wagon contained a family of beautifully colored parrots, then Rakim used his wagon to transport a cage of mongoose. Hakim marched proudly carrying his pet rooster Chuck.

Almost every student in class had or borrowed an animal to be part of the parade. Towards the end of the parade, Daley and his dad drove up in the Mazda truck which was carrying a hundred gallon aquarium containing a fabulous array of sea stars, Angelfish and other sea creatures. The viewing crowd was spellbound! Finally, the very last entry was Amy-Lou with her own calf, Bessie Belle. As they proceeded up the street, the crowd began to laugh and clap wildly.

Bessie Belle wore a sign that read "The End" which was neatly tied to her tail.

After the parade, Mrs. Swanson led all of her students to assemble their pets around the school's yard so that parents and visitors could take a closer look, interview the parade participants and take pictures. While students were busy being interviewed by visiting media folks, the parents were scurrying around preparing the reception. They'd provided sandwiches, pizza, soft drinks, prize bags, as well as certificates and medals for every parade participant. What a jolly celebration everyone was having!

"But, when will the animals be fed?" Henry asked suddenly.

Just then, Mr. Brimager from the local pet shop pulled up in his truck.

"Saw you all's parade! What a hoot! What a terrific idea, Kids", he stated.

"My sons and I figured all of those animals might be needing some lunch about now!" Then he and his sons voluntarily fed every animal, then quickly disappeared back down the road.

As the excitement of the day began to finally calm down, Mrs. Swanson made an unexpected announcement. "Thank you all for coming to our first ever animal parade. It was a great success thanks to all of you. Thanks to my class of wonderfully creative students for actually planning and putting this event together. And thanks to everyone who contributed in some way. Now for my surprise! Because my students did so very well as parade organizers and participants, it has been decided that you may all be dismissed early today. You're all free to go home now!"

"Hooray! Hooray!" they all cheered.

"We had a great parade!" Hakim declared.

"Yeah! It was the best animal parade ever!" exclaimed Makeba.

THE END

Jazzy Jojo

About the Author

Originally from Baltimore, Maryland. Received Associates Degree in Human Services. Service to children and youths include previous experience as a Youth Advocate in Maryland, seventeen years as a Jr. Kindergarten Instructor for USVI preschools, 20 years as an After School / Summer Camp Tutor and Performing Arts Counselor. Most recent 15 years were spent working with students in Kindergarten through 6th grades as a classroom Paraprofessional and Recess Arts and Science Club Organizer for Virgin Islands Public Schools. Mrs. Saunders has received numerous Community Foundation of the Virgin Islands Awards for her service to the islands' children, including the Silverbells & Cockleshells award of 2000 for her work as Performing Arts Specialist for the St. Thomas' and St. John's VI Resources Center for the Disabled's summer and after school programs. Most recently, Mrs. Saunders received annual monetary awards from the CFVI's Anderson Family Teacher's Grants from 2008-2017, as well as AT&T STEM Grants for 2015 & 2016.

Printed in the United States
By Bookmasters